I0682906

Poems in the Key of C#

Phil Caterino

LOST CABIN PRESS

Steamboat Station - Nevada

Copyright

This is a work of fiction. All characters appearing in this work are fictitious and any resemblances to actual people living, dead or in purgatory, are purely coincidental. Meander along with me if you want and trust me, it will take time but there is order here, very faint, but very human.

No part of this book may be reproduced in any manner, without the written permission, except by a newspaper, magazine reviewer or educator who wishes to quote brief passages in connection with a review or classroom assignment.

All rights reserved. Copyright 2021 by Phil Caterino

LIBRARY OF CONGRESS
Control Number: 2021900686

Caterino, Phil, 1951-
Poems in the Key of C#: poems / by Phil Caterino

ISBN # 978-0-578-24433-4

Lost Cabin Press
Post Office Box 17372
Steamboat Station-Nevada-89521

Contents

*They say the
earth vibrates
at 7.83Hz
the wavelength
of C#*

Poetry
is what they call
my pile of words
This heap that litters
my mind

I tried
standing on the peaks
And yelling them out loud
To no avail

Relief however
is in writing
them down
Expunging them
from my brain
Relieving the recurring
repetition of a movie
running in a loop

The poems
are pictures without paint
my way of vomiting words
out of my brain
into yours

Without much pain
involved
   I hope

Mountain Spoke a Cloud

Tinker

He was a roofer
in the summer
Worked on the mountain
in the winter

Feeling bad enough
to go to the clinic
Doc sent him home
diagnosed as a
bad case of indigestion
Maybe those spicy nachos
he had for lunch

Tinker sat down on his sofa
had a heart attack and died

After the funeral
we fought over his skis
while the roofing tools
went unattended

The Shortest Route to Mount Hubris

In a rude shove
on this narrow trail
they raced past us
Leaving us in a cloud of fine dust

Dr. Rudy turned to me
I guess they wanted the route
all to themselves

By the time we got to the
Base of the face
The sun was over the ridge
Warming the granite spire

As we scoured the sunlit face
there wasn't a soul to be found
There was a pack by the lone pine
near the shadows on the ledge
I pointed
with a nod to Dr. Rudy

They went up the wrong gully
that dead ends to a blank wall
with no holds
Dr. Rudy chuckled

Three pitches later
up high enough for a view
it warmed up enough
To shed a layer

We could hear voices

Yelling
Complaining
of being pelleted
by rock dislodged

In our dangling dance
On this glimmering granite

It was the lost boys

They are apparently
suffering from
        Anal Cranial Inversion
Dr. Rudy chuckled

As he scattered a just a little more rock
In our dangling dance on this
Glimmering granite

Mountain as the Face of God

At times I drop to my knees
In prayer
Overwhelmed by this
creation that lay before me
And other
times
I stand on the peaks and shout at
God

Words suspended
in the silence of the
evening sky

Filling the empty
for miles around

100 Singing Nuns

It had snowed
Four feet overnight
And no one wanted
To be the first one
Shoveling

Curly crawled out of his
Bedroom that morning
Toss a few sugar cubes in
A cup of stale coffee
And reheated it

      You put those in your coffee
      The ones on that pink plate

We were his guides
for the rest of the day
And into the night
Before we fell asleep

He came down as
We woke up in the morning
No one had
Shoveled the walkway
      yet
      it was
      life altering
Curley said

He realized in
His Trip
That all of the sounds
In the universe
are made by
100 singing nuns

that are in a room
on Venus

Walks on the Lake Bottom

In the Cave of Wonders
He walks on the bottom of the lake
That is what the elder said of him

He needs protection
          maybe
How does he do this without harm

He found the cave one day
not so much as wandering down the trail
but the stench of urine and
rotting garbage

The rock formation rose above
the smell transcended
His eyes rose to the multi color lichen
Stata that appeared
Halo like above him

Small children play
in the water underneath
As he walks on the lake bottom

Too Tall Tom

We would watch them
On the walls
Pondering how
they made such
a climbing mismatch
Work

Tom was the tall one
just like my climbing partner
and I was just like Yvon
The short one

How did he reached the protection
that his partner would put in
there were times I would
have to jump up
Scraping granite
Suspended over death
  Don't fall
  Don't fall
Running circles around my head

one evening
as the chatter around
the Camp 4 fire grew dim
I asked him how
did he make that work

  It's the challenge
  It makes me a better climber

He spoke

Alpine County

On nobody's radar
Since 1864

In the whole county
not even a stoplight
only a handful of people

Outsiders thought it
was ripe for the picking

First gay activists
from San Francisco
tried to take it over
Posse Comitatus
Tried too
To no avail

Oh
But then
developers came

In the courthouse
that towering clock
a heavy bronze pendulum swung
above the judge's bench

slowly mesmerizing

    tick-tock   tick-tock   tick-tock

The fancy lawyers
with fancy cars
from the Bay
came for the trial

     tick-tock   tick-tock   tick-tock

The fancy lawyers
laughed as they looked
at the empty chairs in
the jury box
No jurors had shown

The judge said
to the sheriff
        go across the street
        over to the Cutthroat Saloon
        Drag everyone out
        And bring them over here

     tick-tock   tick-tock   tick-tock

The fancy lawyers cackled
        its 8:30 in the morning
        We will be back in the Bay by lunch

     tick-tock   tick-tock   tick-tock

Past their fancy cars
through the tall dark oak doors
the sheriff paraded a dozen drunken jurors
into the Courthouse

     tick-tock   tick-tock   tick-tock

Beefsteak Tomatoes

Her friend asked
>Is that laundry hanging
>above your tomatoes

>they are Tibetan prayer flags

You know
>to scare the birds away

>*Oh*

she said
>I didn't know that birds are scared
>of Tibetans

Eulogy in Flip Flops

His daughter asked me
if I would give the eulogy
He was the smartest man I had ever known
      was what I told
the reporter in town that wrote his obit
in the terms of his generation
Leo was a classy guy
How could I give his eulogy
I thought

In flip flops and shorts
We left the mountains
in the ink dark morning
for the drive to the Ocean

as accompanying entourage
Our funeral attire hung
neatly pressed
on hangers
in the car

We drove for four hours
telling Leo stories
sharing 30 years of
      water
      mountains
      insanity of bureaucracy
      billionaires chasing millionaires out of town
      starving the character out of what was once
      a spirited place of characters

we arrived early for the service

in the cool shade
of a grove of towering redwoods
Leo's daughter greeted us
With a smile

      Don't worry we clean up good

      Oh no
she said
      Dad would have wanted you just like you are

      please

So I stood next to the priest
In baggies and flip flops
choking back tears
      humbled
to try to explain what he meant to me

Leo was about what was right for the world
      Everything he did
      Every meeting
      Every hearing
      Every testimony
      Every conversation
Was about what was right for the world

And the eulogy there among
the towering giants that day
      Was right

Crag Lake

On the trail
to Crag Lake
in Desolation Wilderness

a man walks
by
in wingtip dress shoes
carrying a suitcase
a large one
at that

on the trail
through the dust
just
like any
other
backpacker

Dwight

He turned to us
stuck his cigar in his mouth
shifted his
Jaguar convertible into gear
drove away
in a rumble cloud
of grey granite dust

      Environmentalists
      can drive sports cars
He would lambast

Turning eighty today
      will probably quit skiing
      and think about getting a vasectomy

East Slope School

Painted Word
Written Word
Spoken Word

A show
of words

Carvin Marvin

I had never
raced before

Standing on the
Top of the mountain
frozen slope of
randomly placed
bamboo gates
Below
littered the hill
limbs that
looked like
Toothpicks
just like Marvin's
legs

     Any tips
I asked him

     Yeah
     Point your tips
     Downhill
Marvin said

A big frozen
wad of snot
dangling from
his nose

Come Los Ricos

We were perched
around the campfire
As the storm approached
spitting rain on us

Jealously
looking at
Shiny Campers
in behemoth
Shiny Motorhomes

In Mexico
the poor say
that when there's lightning
the rich think that
God is taking their picture

We all laughed
but
Flinched
when the thunder
boomed

Face Our Fears

I was scraping skin
on granite
When I froze
on this tiny ledge

Yvon looking up
from the belay
        laughed and laughed

        the insidious effect of fear
He told me later

Since they hide
in the deepest
and most obscure corners
of our souls
It takes courage
to face our fears

Don't be afraid
because the better version
of yourself
lies in the darkness
face it
it will come out
to the light
        And shine as never before

Frank the Marine

I first noticed the Purple Heart
On his car's license plate
Frank my new neighbor
      said he was an
      endurance runner

When I ask Tim
What that was
He told me
      That is someone that runs a long way

Tim was an ultra-runner
      Not much difference
he spoke
A few hundred miles here or there

It's a small tight community of
ultra-runners
      yeah
      I know him
Tim said
didn't know his name
we all call him
      the Marine

The marine's wife
came over around sunset
worried about Frank
He went for a run
didn't come back

Frank just told her he was

Going for run
Be back in a while
        Don't worry
I told the marine's wife
        I'll check around
        hospitals
        police
        park rangers
        local strip club

I saw the marine's wife
coming and going all night

The next day she stops her car
rolling down the window
        I going to kill that guy
        He didn't want me to know
        because
        I would not
        have let him

Frank the Marine
had taken off
to run the
an endurance race
100 miles and 19 hours later
He called from a payphone
in California
Asked If she would come
and pick him up

At 68 Frank just wanted to know
If he could still do it

        Race
I asked him

No
Sleep on the sofa for weeks

Full Moon Fireworks

We sat on the crowded
Beach
Kids kicking sand clouds
in the dusk
As the full moon rose
over the mountains

As if in perfect alignment with the gods
the explosions of colour
framed that moon sphere
which rotates around us

it may be the fourth of july
instead it could have been a
Lunar Birthday Party

We all looked at each other
as the fireworks moon
came to visit us

One evening in the mountains
it all came together

Hangtown California

I told him I lived in
>Hangtown

He nervously laughed
>You messing with me

>No

Who would live in place called Hangtown
>*I mean*

>What was hanging

>People

>People

>Who would hang people

Why did they do that

>They thought it was a proper punishment

For what
>Being people

Well not anymore at least

>Maybe

Jack Rabbit Moon

January 20th
I woke up this morning
To a jack rabbit eating
Breakfast under
the full moon as it
set in the
red sky morning

This was the year of the rabbit
I thought
the first rabbit moon of the
the year

Framed in my window

Koopmans Corner

There is no sign
but everyone knows
its name

As we came around the
Icy curve
that is always in the
shade of the
Mountain

Tire tracks
carved through
the snow bank
car upside down in
the ravine
Snow covered
Icy bound

Koop crawling up a
Blood stained
snowy slope
like someone
tie dyed it

Lam wat tah

the Elder laughed
> we are not as young
> As we were

> And we can't run as
> Fast as we use to

> So now we must
> Ask permission
> for our
>> Trespasses

Later That Evening

We drove into Hangtown
To play a party

A bunch of Clampers
Showed up
jumped up
On stage
guns drawn

       Keep playing boy
they said

As they took over the mikes
And blew
Off key harmonicas
       Into the drunken audience

Naked Cowboy

DB was standing there
butt naked
high as a kite

On the bank
of the American River
at the bend
before Troublemaker

With only his holster
and six shooter on

While rafts full
of people coming
by on white water
are sucked into a time gone by

Where naked cowboys
     Ruled the river

Path of Snow

I am a pilgrim on the path of snow
      Skins on, skins off
I am a pilgrim on the path of snow
      Wax on, wax off
I am a pilgrim on the path of snow
      Klister on, klister off
I am a pilgrim on the path of snow
      Skins on, skins off
      I am a pilgrim
           on the path
of snow

Repeat for seven days till
    you have reached
               the Big Trees
                Pilgrim

Pyramid Peak

As we climbed toward
the talus strewn
Summit

A bearded man
in flip flops
Comes walking down

Like Jesus
Descending upon high
without a word and only
A smile
he passes us

That night we slept
On the summit
In a coffin of talus stone

I wasn't sure if
It was dream as
A shooting star blew
By
Almost within reach

Sandpaper Wind

The perpetual
dust gusts and zephyrs
blows the sandpaper grinder
the timing is
Merciless

just when you approach
the intersection
You never notice
until just the right angle
of late afternoon
Winter sun
Refracts it

Splintering
a thousand prisms
Exploding before the desert
and blinds you in a second

Every little pit in the glass
Mesmerizing you
as you drive off the road

In a car with the
Nevada windshield

Raccoon Prints

Every morning
that summer
I would wake up
To their tiny little paw prints
across the top and over the hood
of my car
a little
coon calling card
Left for me

Much nicer than
Stellar Jays
that would squawk
at me
before I even had coffee

And then
crap on my windshield

Rexroth's Guide to Camping

As one reads
the unpublished Rexroth
He makes you feel
a part of an infinitely interrelated
complex of being

you think of yourself as a
microcosm and macrocosm

You become related to chipmunks
       Bears
       Pine trees
       Stars
       Nebulae
       Rocks
       Fossils

maybe
       distantly related

Song Bird

The small
most dull
looking of birds
Has a voice of many colors

plain and tiny
projecting the most amazing voice
heard on the mountain
It doesn't need to boast

Echoing through the canyon
Ravines and Ridges
this song of many colors and depth
Echoes through the canyon
Cascading down
down
To the sands of the desert below
      The Josephs' coat of birds

Running Talus

That summer
I wanted to learn
to rock climb
but all he did was have us
Run up and down the
Talus field all day

      Run up
Run down
      Run up
Run down

      Grasshopper

When the warmth of the granite
had turned cold in
the shadow of winter

I danced from ledge to ledge
Upward to the summit
the epiphany of running talus

      Grasshopper

Scar Tissue

At what point
do your scars
Lead you to a
Realization

that moving
onwards
Is not
an only solution
But is in accordance
with what should be just
In the world

That scar tissue
is stronger
than regular tissue
Realize the strength
        Move on

Speeding Ticket

       In a hurry
Why do cops always say that
       No
       I just like to drive fast on mountain roads
Why did I say that
       Not in my town
Why do cops always say that

       Go to the old stone library in town to pay it
He said

The librarian
Slowly shuffles
from the book section
through the non-fiction aisle
       to the ticket paying section
       of the library
And takes your money

looking over the top of her glasses
       Cash only
       Son
Says the librarian

Tallac

That dog was on guard duty
from the day he was born

No matter where the family was
He was always
on point
positioned
To watch everything
that was going on

A week after Tallac had died
In my arms at the vet
My son was
emptying the dishwasher
With a big smile
he pulled out his dog bowl
When with the falling weight
of a anchor in the Bay
He realized
that he would not be eating
from that bowl
Anymore

He rose up and lifted that anchor
With a wish that Tallac's hunger
would now be fulfilled by
the Heaven For Dogs
that he surely now resided in

Law and Order

My friend
was dating the
Superintendents'
Daughter

A reprieve from
the dirt and dust
of the campground
to get invited to the
Rangers and Bears BBQ

We could look
right up at the
Lost Arrow
from the Supe's Backyard
watching our friends
dangle while we
munched on ribs

      Here comes the judge
      Here comes the judge
The gathering would repeat
In a friendly but mocking chant
As the dark breaded guy
Came into the backyard

I never realized
that they had their
own judge and jail in the valley
As I stood there
Sweet sticky fingers
with a bag of weed

in my pocket
Later the bears show up
For the sweet-smelling feast

And the evening
Confrontation
would begin
     Law and Order
        Vs
     Wild and Hungry

The Blind Guy on the Wall

He asked me if I would
take him to the wall
      My guide would come along
      of course
Mike said

Mike thinks his skiing has advanced enough
and his guide concurred

Of course if your blind
you can't see the abyss below you
but would you ask a blind friend
to take the wheel on a curvy mountain road

There is an advantage to that concept
your skiing can considerably advance
all righty
It is just that if you fall you might die
or certainly be
a shredded bloody mess at the bottom

Mike went ahead
I lagged behind just in case

Years later he after a surgery
that restored his sight
I talked with him
he laughed
that now when
he could see the wall
he thanked me for tagging along
      but questioned my judgement

Great Ocean of Truth

The shaman stood
before the salty water

Only yesterday I was
but a boy playing on the shore
Looking for little things to pluck
Place or toss
Always diverting myself in looking for something
other than ordinary
       While before me
       with the ocean
       lay all the truth
       I would ever need

For the tribe had a word for the
Salty water
Because some have traveled
       to the land of the beginning
       Where our waters flow into
       the salty water

Lollipop Tree

A mile down the dirt road
through stands of pine and oak
scraping manzanita in the corners
through six hairpins
just to reach my house
Next to it
standing on top of a high dry hill
Overlooking the
American River Canyon
stood one solitary digger pine

relentless winds on this
Lofty perch
had shorn it of limbs along
Its lanky trunk
only its crown survived
a crown of branches resembling
A lollipop

It wasn't till many years had passed
that I found out that
It was a navigation landmark
for many of the river guides

Knowing that
following the siting of the
Lollipop Tree
          they were in for it

Ahead the rapids
known as Troublemaker

Sweet

The Ancient One

Reaching out to touch this
4,000 year old tree

wishing it could speak
in words
instead of Branches
Cones and Needles

Waterbabies

What you do
to meet
the Waterbabies

you go to the bottom of the lake
where the water isn't blue anymore
where the sky is just a memory
and float there
in the silence and wait
and if you decide you would die for the lake
only then
will they come out

and greet you
and judge the love
you have for the lake
and if you are sincere in your love
they will be with you forever

to be held in their arms
to be held by the lake

Tuolumne Dust

We met up with
Frank Smokey in
Tuolumne Meadows

We cooked a chicken
On the coals
While kids raised
thick dust
in the camp

He told us how the word for
goodbye in MiWuk is
      there are no farewells

As he ate the chicken off of his plate

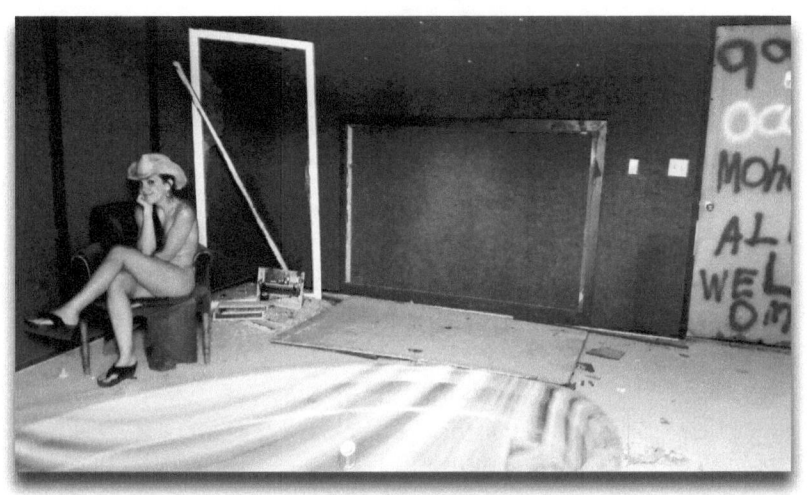

Lahontan Ladies

Sandi

Some Women will test you

Drunk on Thanksgiving
Emergency Room
third degree Burns
from the turkey grease

Face first in the
Breakfast Huevos
at the Freel Peak Saloon

Middle of the night
driving down the summit road
seeing her car crashed up
against a pine tree

Walking out of the
Penthouse Elevator
with her blouse
on inside out

Gloria

Wake Up
Wake Up

Get out of bed
She yelled at us

Rest when you're dead
Get out of bed

Dee

We were all standing
around at the Swim Center
waiting for the
Instructor to unlock the door
for the lifesaving class

Red hair blazing
She screamed into the parking lot
In a beat-up Volkswagen
Twenty minutes late

Red hair blazing
cracked open the car door
a dozen empty beer cans
rolled out clinking
Onto the parking lot

white legs followed the
beer cans out the door
already wearing her swimsuit
she casually picked up all the cans and threw
them back in through the broken
rear window

Red hair blazing
we all didn't know what was scarier
the milk white skinned
blazing haired
bathing beast
herself

or what
she might have
in store for us in the class

Later that week
swerving up the
mountain road
to the pass
I saw Dee
driving
Red hair blazing
through
the bug stained
windshield

I skidded off the road
and parked
A heartbeat away
From drowning

A Split Heart Hoof

Onto the soft earth a doe's split heart hoof fell
Crushing the green vegetation, repeatedly breaking
it roots, its presence pushed to the side, a path
emerges

My daughter looked down
At the track in the mud

What is that

It is a deer track

It looks like a heart but broken

Like two lovers
That have fallen apart
She speaks

Do you think they got divorced

Hope Faith & Charity

Hanging between the mountains
three beautiful valleys

      Each divided by towering walls of granite
      Each unique
      Each flowing water
      Each flowering a meadow

Join at a point
where they meander together
As one
      Three sisters
      from one mother

Fisherwoman's Tree

It looked just like the trees
I saw on the ridge at
Star Lake

In the middle of winter
A huge avalanche
off the flanks
of Freel Peak
White thundering force
breaking through the thick
ice of Star Lake

Creating the great wave
ice water and snow
Hurling through frozen air
so that
There
hundreds of feet beyond the shore
Frozen trout
Festooned the pine boughs
like Christmas decorations
On a fisherman's tree

It looked just like that
I thought winters later
Again

Behind the lodge at
Fallen Leaf
a pond maintained
for fire fighting
With trout planted

by the caretaker
for her dinner

   Nothing to see here
She said to me

As I walked past the
Trout festooned
boughs of the
Fisherwomen's
Christmas Tree

Sweaty Betty

She rented us a cabin
in back of her house
Betty didn't know we
were still in high school

She thought we were
nice enough kids
That paid in cash

a poor man's
Elizabeth Taylor
all dolled up with
Red lipstick
Hair to the ceiling
each wrist dangling with
junk store jewelry

Like a mom
she looked over us
Having no idea we were
dealing weed out of her yard

a stoned client
Smashed into her
mailbox one day

She stood up from
the White Wicker chair
on her porch
cocktail in hand

    Damn

she said
And sat back down

Olga

She grew up so poor

In a corrupt
communist regime
Her way out
was to be a ballerina

Even though
her parents
were both doctors
They were paid in cabbage
      Growing up
      You never forget that kind of thing
she would say

When we went out for dinner
She always ordered the
      Most expensive meal
      Most expensive wine
on the menu
Even if she didn't like it
or even know what the hell it was

Because now
she wouldn't
Have to pay with cabbage

One day stopping at a saloon
in a little town in the mountains
we walked in through
a thick jungle canopy of bras hanging
from the dark smoke-stained ceiling

Biker chicks had tacked hundreds
of their bras up

in astonishment
Olga stopped dead and gasped
           What is wrong with these women
That they would toss away
Such a valuable commodity

In an epiphany
throwing her long blond hair
Back
it was not the
consummate act of
Retaliation
to some feminist dogma
Or maybe
just some sluty
provocations

To Olga
like the menu
it was a show of contempt for
those cocksuckers that paid
her parents with cabbage

In a ballerina like swope
she whipped off her bra
and flung it at the
Bartender

As every cowboy in the bar
grabbed the tip of their hat

Flo's Dream

My aunt called me
Sobbing
      she was so sorry

She had the strangest dream
Michael was showing her a new watch
upon his wrist
      Saying don't worry
      I got a new watch now
      Isn't it nice

Aunt Flo lives in Florida
My brother died
in a plane crash
In Utah

I flew to Utah
to receive his remains
I remember
that all the pieces left
were in one body bag
that the distressed
Sheriff's deputy
had on the gurney

      I'm so sorry
the deputy said

looking down
he fidgeted
with his keys on his belt
      it was the worst crash I ever worked

All I found
small pieces of my brother
a mangled wedding ring
and lying at the bottom
of the black rubber
Body bag
mixed with hair and blood
        A broken watch

Foxi

No one at the University
had realized that we had
built illegal apartments
at the Sculpture Lab

It was a huge two story
metal building
Next to the American River
on the outskirts
of the campus
Foxi had converted the corner
room on the first floor

For some reason the University
thought it was a good idea to
bring the Governor and his
entourage to the
Sculpture Lab
for a tour while on campus

A gaggle of dark suits
like penguins on a shore
stood in wonder looking at one
of the massive Corten sculptures
squatting on the floor

Foxi walked out of her room
Disheveled hair
Brushing her teeth
in a beat-up paint-stained bathrobe

Walking casually by

the group of penguins
to the rust-stained work sink

spit out a foaming glop
of white sputum
walked back into her apartment
and slammed the door

You could feel the silence
even though the sound
from Foxi's door slamming
was still echoing off the
metal walls of the cavernous building

One of the Governor's aides
looked down at his clipboard
        so briefly
And announced
        Next on the schedule is the tour of the
        new Physics Building
        Governor

Bethany

Like the Black and White Island
soaking
in the hot springs
nakie pool

The Sawtooths
in the background
as the heat seeps into your body
Each breast raised up
caked with black and white
sulfur mud

      Look
she said
      it's like
      the black and white islands
      we saw at the salty lake
As she stared at her chest

We floated on
that short walk
Back to the car
      Sulfur mud splattered
      On the little Alfa's
      floor mats

Katie

She sat there
in her tiny tank top
and cutoffs
In the summer heat
of the valley

with the huge
White Plaster
dildo shape between
her pale thin legs

plaster casts
we made
for our installation
at the art show

Gazing
from the other studio room
stood Larry
mesmerized
cutting stained glass
for his sculpture

His blood
in small drips
splattering red stains
on the concrete
floor of the studio

Wesleyan Wolf Choking Association

He was playing with
Bubba Din Muk
the dog from Morocco
who looked like a wolf

Drunk as a skunk
Sandi turned to me
      he looks like he is choking that dog
      make him stop

      I can't
I said
      It is part of the initiation
      to belong to the Association

      Oh
she slurred

      He not hurting him
      is he

      No you can choke a wolf till
      They pass out
      and then they wake up
      Bubba will be fine

      Oh
she slurred

Parents Return

Nestled in bed
young dumb and
full of cum
The phone rang

Her brother
down the street
saw her parents
drive by
a day early

Naked I ran
with a wad of clothes
out the back
through the sunroom
into the yard

with a
Leap of faith
Over
the back fence

Catching my breath
such a close call
I chuckled
made it

Embarrassment
then shame
To follow as
I turned to see
I had forgot her fence

bordered
the neighborhood park

Mothers and kids
on picnic blankets
Stared
drop mouthed

Slowly
but deliberately
I dress myself
and casually walked down
the park path

Past picnic blankets
Retrieving my dignity
          of sorts

Mavis Jean

I met you last
Saturday night
at Steve's Bar & Grill
My introduction was
a $20 bill

don't you know
your prescription needs filled
Mavis Jean and her pills
determined so
to run that body
down hill

I love you Saturday night
you were looking so fine
come Sunday morning
it's curlers pills and wine

don't you know
that prescription needs filled
Mavis Jean and her reds
passed out in her bed

The Contessa

She made
the biggest mess
out of the nicest guys

She looked like
she was ridden hard
and put away wet
So many times

like
my barn sour mare
named Sugar

Tamale Lady

Every Friday afternoon
She comes
knows we get paid on Fridays

has handmade Tamales
  beef
  chicken
  cheese
  and chile rellenos

in her tender hands
made with love

with each purchase
she gives a small amount of her sauce
wrapped in a plastic bag
and knotted tight
a sauce so
exquisite and fiery
that Satan ponders jealously
up from hell

quietly making the rounds
through all the
cubicles of the office
  cash only
pulling change
from a well-worn purse

making enough to pay the rent
or the utility bill
they don't even know her name,

everyone just calls her
the Tamale Lady

the ladies at the front desk
tell me her only son
was killed in Iraq

I wondered if those that sent him there
sell tamales to
pay for their estate
in the Hamptons

Thunder's Daughter

Thunder sent his daughter
to live in the hills for a year

To fend for herself
to make her strong
With only her dog Bark
as a companion

For nearly a year she
cohabitated with
　　　　mountain lions
　　　　coyotes
　　　　wild horses
　　　　and burros

The authorities found out one day
and made her come back into town
and go to school like the other kids

She was amazed
that the other kids were
so cruel to her

　　　Why would they do that
she asked Thunder

　　　　That is why I sent you to live in the mountains,
　　　　the mountains can be cruel at times
　　　　but they are beautiful also
　　　　the mountains do not judge
　　　　a balance exists
　　　　People are never beautiful

I never have seen a totally sane human being
One day
Enough

Thunder's Daughter
caught a sack full of bull snakes

She put them in everyone
of her tormentors
lockers at school

No one ever bothered
Thunder's daughter again

This is what happens
when you mess
with a girl
that has cohabitated
        with mountain lions

Sweetwater Town

In the evening
when the sun goes down
I'll catch her running around
this Sweetwater Town

The lights
at the end of the pier
that shimmer on clear water
Mesmerize her
to drink herself crazy
like a drowning fool
Diving to the bottom
and never coming up

You think your holding
the good hand
but the
drugs and drinks
Cloud your cards

You should pack your bags
and leave this town
For the water is sweet
but your friends
like fools are
busting up furniture
to fuel the fire

there is
      No rent and
      No real friends
In this Sweetwater Town

Christine

She can change your flat
and write you a song

She wanted to walk around
the lake that afternoon
before her show

I showed her the lake
and we barely had time
to tune her guitar

Then she played
The Good You Do
for me

Nonni

I had a girlfriend
Who had a horse

She spent all her time
with that damn horse

If I wanted to see her
I had to go over to the stables
in the dust and dung
was where she always hung

Frustrated with horse love
I went and signed up to
Go to Vietnam
          I will show her

old high school
football injury
failing the physical
I stayed at home
While politicians
sent my friends to die
in some jungle swamp

I felt no gratitude
when her horse threw her
Broke her arm

years later
we met up and I
thanked her for the thing
she never knew she did

And we wept
for our friends
that politicians
sent to die
in some
jungle swamp

Don't Drink and Drive Lady

I saw her every morning
At the intersection
along the highway

with her hand made sign
Held above her head for
Every motorist to see

Please don't drink and drive

For a year she was there
In the rain and the snow

I wanted so to stop and talk
But at the time I couldn't take
Any more pain and
she had some to share
With her sign of lost love

I never stopped
I told myself
      That intersection is
      Too dangerous
      Too crowded
      Too narrow
      Too old
      Too too

One day she was gone
To share her pain
st another intersection
Where paths cross

Nina

A foreign exchange student
She came from Sweden
to
Teach all the boys
a lesson

A Viking
looting and plundering
The Virgin boys
of California

Andrea

A brilliant mind
in med school
as a teenager

She was desperately in love with him
but lacking
in functional relationship skills

How do I keep him
She asked Loraine

The wrong girl to ask
The wrong girl to give
advice
Just suck his dick
Quipped Loraine

Relentless weeks of
Oral pleasure consumed
their relationship

But could not hold sway over
a psychotic malfunction of
that spark
between them

One day he left
Driving away
in Loraine's car

Chee

Chee use to hide
in jungle highlands
From the Viet Cong

Now she hides
behind a pile of peaches
in her stall
at the Farmers Market

this Hmong Farmer
from the Sacramento Valley
turns the fruit around
on the crate
hiding any imperfections

       Chee means shining in Hmong
Chee says
       But I am not as bright as I use to be

She laughs
Looks at my daughter

       She beautiful girl
       Children
       they are all
       from same tree
       but each one
       is so different

Waving her small wrinkle hand
Over her crate of perfect peaches
       Just like my fruit

The Loving Couple

The Brand Inspector
took them away today
Together

They have always been together
as long as I have seen
Them on the edge of town

Our ranch sits between
the open range
and suburbia
a buffer between
the wild kingdom and
the riot of people

only wanting some sweet green grass
Not the bitter brown weeds of the
High Range

They probably were not even wild
Just left behind
Abandoned by their owners
Who lost their homes and jobs and life
just turned them out to the wild
they don't know about cars
streets or leaf blowers

The horse ladies try to help as best they can
hundreds of them left to wander
with everyone against them

They took them away today

Together

The loving couple
Will die together
Far from sweet grass of home
In a slaughterhouse
That men built

The Red River Girl

The rest of the song
is a poem
she said

And rode her horse
across the creek
Taking the air with her

Stephani

Stephani waits for me
by the oak near
Hangman's Creek

While the bay horse
plays
she waits all day
Waiting in
Satin and
in Lace

Wrapped in harmony
She is a singing jay
I can't go
I can't stay

The Koyukon Kennel Klub

Yeah
Yeah
Yeah
he said

No

You
You
You

Pointing at him
Bai said in broken English through
The few teeth left in her mouth

What are you going to do about those dogs
You lazy man
I can't even hang laundry out
without being
Accosted

Yeah
Yeah
Yeah
he said
Dogs Bark

Waiting with Bear

I fumbled with the
Lines on my boat
As she walked by

Standing on the dock
At the marina
Corrina flirted with me
With the biggest beautiful eyes
I've ever seen

I get off at 11
She smiled

She worked at the
Cantina
A popular place
In town

I sat in the only
Empty stool at the bar
Started up a
Conversation with a
Big burly bearded guy
Whose name was Bear

As he talked
I moved my stool
a little
to get a glimpse
of Corrina as she
came up to the bar
to get her orders

I'm waiting for my wife
To get off work
the beard said
I going to surprise her tonight

We joked and talked
as Corrina came up to the bar
with an order
the bartender partially blocking
her from view
but I saw those big beautiful eyes
almost burst through
her skull
as she looked up
her face grew pale

Hi Babe
Said Bear

and those
biggest beautiful
eyes

Terrifying Beauty

Mike had a promising
racing career
Broke his leg at
the finish line
then he met Julianna

She was a beauty with
Flowing long black hair across
Her breasts

She was one of those women
who could bend a decent man
Bend him like a twig
and bring him to his knees

She had that look
Rough around the edges
but not enough to think
she might not be a beauty
After all
Thinly disguised as a woman
who cared
Dark eyed
Liquor
wafted from her nostrils

Walking Away

You have to walk away
No strings attached
Do you know what that means

You have to walk away from her
like walking off a cliff

Walking into mud
stuck to your heart instead
of your feet

The Wildflower Lady

When you visited Toni
at her cabin
You had to
walk through the bathroom
to get to her kitchen

Such a lovely lady
She was the only
person that would
talk Latin with me

She knew that Carson Pass
was the center of the
great horseshoe
of flowers
That bends around
Hope Valley
Jobs Sister
ending at Mt. Rose

Often as we hiked
she would
Bend down low
and squint
     Arnica latifolia
     Rare
     Found only in rock crevice
     wet with seepage

Dominus Vo Biscum, Toni
Dominus Vo Biscum

Going to See a Man About a Horse

Dread of Making Mistakes

One hand
Softly on her neck
The other on the bridle

She turned to me

> You allow a horse to make mistakes
> the horse will learn from mistakes

Different than the human
where you dread making mistakes
for fear of the consequences

Some imagined
Some very real

Mentor

It is the small things
that change people's lives

I was too young and dumb
To realize it at the time

Like poets rub words
together with verse

Like musicians that
Rub notes together
in a song

He taught me to rub
colors together
on linen

A Glimpse of Elvis

Working evening shift
in the casino kitchen
at the Sahara

Standing there
holding onto a garbage can
of chicken carcass stench

the double doors to kitchen
  swung open
   Two big thugs
with big thug rings on their fingers
Burst through into the kitchen

One grabbed my garbage can
and flung it to the side
the other thug grabbed me
and flung my little ass
On top of the garbage can
of chicken carcass stench

Looking up from my new vantage point
more big thugs with big thug rings
Burst in
Surrounding him as they
Whisked through the kitchen
to the stage corridor

For an instance
The King looked down
at poor poor pitiful me
lying in a stew
of chicken carcasses stench

Encina

Pattitucci loved that wooden sculpture
on the art department plaza

One day Aron
stoned on hash
thought his truck
was in reverse

collapsed it in a heap of splinters

It was the only time I ever
saw Joe cry

Almost Accident

I was staring
wth a stopped truck in the way
I almost turned into the oncoming
Traffic

In a split second of time
the whole accident flashed
Through my mind
> Vivid
> Crashing
> Banging
> Screaming
> Ambulance
> Hospital
> Doctors
> Repair shop

But I stopped
in time
and missed
the whole
Accident

Rattled
I pulled over
to the side of the road
Catch my breath
and senses

I grabbed my balls
to make sure I wasn't
Dreaming

Painter of Flagpoles

Did you find someone to paint those flagpoles

> Yes
> he is a flagpole painter

> Oh
> Like his business card reads
> Joe the flagpole painter
they laughed at me

> No, his name is Sid
> Sid Balustine

He learned to paint flagpoles in the navy
Uses a boatswain chair

Arthritis has made it hard for him to haul himself up
He told me
> but his big belly has made it easier to paint
> It gives him room between the pole and paint
he laughs

As he packed up his rags and paint,
hands me his card

In embossed red ink on a white background

> Sid Balustine
> **Flagpole Painter**

Thunder Road Revisited

We got a summer job
tax mapping for the
State of Georgia

We travelled down
Endless winding woods and roads
Into the hill country to verify boundaries

We had hardly got out of the rental car
when we found ourselves surrounded
by gun toten hill people

We thought
they were all protecting their stills

       Like in the movies racing old souped-up cars
       A trunk full of Moonshine through the hills and
       hollows being chased by the sheriff

About to crap our pants
it's just our job we told them
       Tax mapping these parcels
Fumbling with all the rolled up parcel maps

They didn't seem to care much
       about what we are doing

Guns lowered they are laughing all the way
back to their spanking brand new pickup trucks
Offered to buy us
a drink in town
Well

they seemed nice enough
After a few
this red hair gal on the barstool
her big breasts
Bursting out of her plaid shirt
Kinda cozied up
to the us

      You boys were scare
She twanged

      You thought we were cops looking for your stills
I blabbed out

      Ah
      Boys

As she leaned over far enough
to spill a splash of beer on my pants

      No one moonshines anymore

      The boys there all thought you were Feds
      snooping about for the weed they been growing
She twanged

      Who'd moonshine when you can sell weed to suits in the
city
She twanged

      Ya' all think we are just some cider sucking hicks down
here
      Don't ya
She twanged

putting her hand on my thigh

still damp with spilled beer

Answering Machine

Months after passing away
my Aunt still talks with me

Uncle Rudy keeps her on the
answering machine message

When I call

hear her cadence
see her smile
I can recall
the smell of her
Perfume in each word

Shitty First Draft

I have been working
on this book for six years

Trying to find words
that sing to the heart
lines that snap together
in the reader's mind
like pieces of a puzzle

I work to
painstakingly craft
some intellectual
emotional movement
within the reader

Try as I might
It's still a pretty
shitty first draft

for Annie

He Got Hit by a Car

While her dad's health
was deteriorating
A stray dog got hit by a car
in front of the house

      Bloody
      mangled
      remains of a dog
Left for dead
      In the dirt
      on the
      side of the road

Her father insisted
      take him to the vet

As they nursed him
back to health
she noticed
as the dog recovered
her dad's spirits returned
like youth reincarnate

This pitiful remains of a dog
in a bonding recovery
as they both healed
Soul and Spirit resplendent

Except for a few missing limbs
in the house
It made things like they were again

A sunny day on the porch
sat her Dad and his bulldog with
one eye and three legs
named
I Hop

Red Line of San Miguel de Allende

Shuffling through the terminal
Back from
getting limestone samples
from a quarry in Mexico
we were coming through Customs
with heavy packs of stone

     What is in those
The agent said

Trying too carefully
swing the hefty bundle
Up on the table

It crashed down
In cloud of white dust
covering the agent

As the cloud settled
     Empty your pockets
     Gentlemen
He said
     Please follow the
     Red Line to the room
     Over there
     Where you can undress

     Wait

     It is
     Limestone

Sir please
Follow the *Red Line* on the floor
to the room

Over there
Where you can undress

The Red Line
Sir

Four Kids Came Singing

for weeks
It had been
a bitter dry cold
at Sierra Station

Crack your skin
Bone dry
High Desert cold

Sitting by the fire
the dogs barked

four kids appeared at the door
in the frozen night

their mother standing by the road
In family harmony
they sung
    Hark the Herald Angels Sing
Wished me a Merry Christmas

with a wave of their hands
disappeared
down the road
crackling through frozen air

Every Artist is a Thief

Originality is nothing but judicious imitation
—VOLTAIRE

In class one day
Carlos Villa looked at my work
    I have seen that
he said rubbing his chin

Terrified
    of plagiarism—
      being accused of it
I spewed out
    I borrowed that from Jack

Carlos reprimanded me
    you never borrow anything
    Just steal it

Artists are slowly and ceaselessly
searching for things we can steal
and slightly manipulate it so
as to then pass off as our own

a natty bit of color,
a seamless transition,
a visual metaphor that jumps to its target
like a tick from a bush

Every artist is a thief

though some of us are more clever
than others at disguising how we steal

Droopy Drawers

He was a miner

A coal miner
with black lung

Black lung would make
him cough so loud
he would wake up the
whole neighborhood

He called me
     droopy drawers
Since I was little
because my diapers
would hang down
I had no butt

He made it for awhile
nursed on by a loving wife
and family
He died when I was 8 years old

After the Rosary
I signed his book at the funeral home

Rest in Peace
Your friend
Droopy Drawers

Draft Help

In 1969
I sat on a sofa
that was bent on spewing
its foam guts all over the room
when a shy young pimpled face boy
burst through the beat-up screen door

      I saw your sign
      I wasn't sure if
      I wanted to go to the marines or the army
The kid caught his breath
      I saw your sign
      Draft Help

If you could give me some advice
I would really appreciate it

Before I could get out a word
Lt. Wethers
who had just returned from
two tours in Nam
Stood up
      I can help you son
      Took him into the back room

He emerged later
Pale
Shaken
but with a whole new perspective
      I will think about it
      Lt. Wethers
      Maybe Canada ain't so bad

Deke

Saw Deke at the Rodeo
that kid has busted more
Bones than I know

But in his heart and
in his mind
He's riding tonight
Broken nose
And a few busted toes

Now Deke waved as I
Drove away
Still remembers
those Fort Worth Days
When we were young
and crazy as hell
Working on those wells
Pulling nine to twelves

Now I'm driving
down this interstate
eating lunch
off a paper plate
dragging a lot of
broken weight
over highways
Talladega to the
Golden Gate

While Deke is
Busting broncs
out of a rusted gate

Bob's Black

I was taught
      Forever

You NEVER use Black
for any reason
much less to tint
any color

You were shunned
by color community
if they caught you
with a tube of black paint

Unless you used Bob's Black

     Let me be your color man
He said to me

No one
ever said that to me
No one
in art world wants to
Actually help artists

that ego dwelling
in the bowels of the artworld
is too big

     Yes, let me be your color man
     I will show you how I make paint

As I toured his shop

under Portland Gray skies

His black is like no one else's
he feels the whole world is to
be bathed in his colors

As I slowly tint out
        Alizarin Crimson
with Bob's Black

my old art instructors
Roll over in their graves

Cakebox

He pulled into
The gravel driveway
in a VW dune buggy
powder blue

Painted on the driver's door
was a simple styled cake
with the words
      Cakebox

He had bought
the car from
a lady
who made
and delivered
      Cakes
in Oakland California

But now it was Big Al's ride
With Big wheels and Big tires
And a powder blue door
      Cakebox

Fingers

I talk to her
with my fingers

My mom

Said the deaf boy
In a deaf voice

To the stranger
In line at the grocery store

My mom

I talk to her
With my fingers

Bermuda

In Santa Cruz
one day
I saw a house
in the neighborhood

Lawn chairs set out
      But no lawn
Just sand
and some
      Fake palm trees
      Seaweed
      And flamingos

A handmade sign
From driftwood
      Bermuda

He said he wanted
      Bermuda to be
      with him
      Wherever he went

Who Da Guy

We were standing in the saloon
up against the dark bar
with wood chips
scattered about the floor
Steve looked over at me

Listening to that guy
Barking hubris for what seemed
Forever

He finally walked away
        Who Was that guy
I said

Steve looked over at me
        Who Da Guy
        He was a *whodaguy*
        Wasn't he

Steve nodded
        Who Da Guy

Waiting My Turn for the MRI

I sit with moderate pain
among those
       Dying
        terminally ill
        other beings
        mothers
        sons
        daughters
        and fathers

Surrounded by family
or friends
watching TV
reading the paper
any distraction
from their appointment
with reality

They don't really want the news

may dread the analysis
more than the procedure

I feel ashamed to be
among them
I am just the walking wounded
amongst
those who in the combat of life
are morality wounded
but still endure their crosses

The Whirleys

Mrs. Whirley
she was Kirby's neighbor
 at the Silver Lake cabin

We were on mushrooms
when I met her

I barely survived

The Rich Californian

He bought 40 acres of alfalfa
From old man Dressler
Dink and I were hired to set fence

       I left California it's awful there now
He *said*

       I made a fortune in Donuts and sold the business
       to a bunch of chinks
He *said*

He stretched out his arms
       This is God's country boys
       This is our country
He *said*

a trailer full of high dollar Arabian horses pulled up
and were unloaded into the pasture

Dink looked at me
and stumbled on some words
something like
       You all can't leave those horses
       in that pasture overnight

       What do mean
       This is my ranch now
He *said*

       I am a goddamn rancher
       This is god's country
       I don't listen to ditch diggers

He *rambled on* for awhile
next morning
as I pulled in for work
The sun was just coming up
over the mountains
all I could see from the road
as the bright light
lite the pasture
were rigid legs

their hoofs
in the air like an
Equine Revival Meeting
Reaching for their god
or a centaur

and the
rising dust off the frontage road
as Dink driving a Backhoe
for Burial Duty
bounced down to the pasture

      Hurry up before anyone drives by
The goddamn rancher said

University of Diversity

He was smarter
than most anyone
I had ever met

He had graduated from the most
Prestigious institution in the world

       No sheepskin
       Ceremony
       Tassel
       Ring

He labored with
his hands
in a world that
Academia
doesn't recognize
Or knows exists

Package from Nam

Grunka was our
mixed pound puppy
She was a postman loving dog

She would wait every day
for the postman to come
and follow him around the
Neighborhood

Coming back at the end of
his route one day
the postman
knocked on the door

Apologizing while he
handed me a parcel
wrapped in shredded brown paper

With the return address
>Sgt. Burkett
>101st Airborne
>Da Nang
>Vietnam

So sorry it was damaged before
I got it, I'm so sorry
I think it's your friend in the army

As cannabis wafted out
of the torn corner onto
the front steps
of our house
>*As the war waged on*

Petulant Child

Who is the kid in the painting
She asked me
Oh
that is the petulant child

I just like that word
querulous
is the same
as petulant
but sounds
so
piercing

Gary Decides

Because I live down a dirt road
I have to drive my garbage
to the dump

Every week

Every week
Gary decides
What I will be paying

Every week
It changes

Sometimes a dollar
Sometimes twenty dollars
It depends on how long I will listen
To his rants about
       Government
       Women
       Guns
       Or the vet bills for his dogs tumor

Every week
It was different

Every week

Sometimes I would listen
Cause a dollar is good deal
Sometimes I just couldn't take it
And that cost me

Every week

Throughout the year
More or less
It would go like that

As winter approached
his rants got
darker and deeper
like the mud on my road

One week
I pulled up to the gate
a new bearded garbage guy
in denim overalls
stood under
a newly painted sign
on the dump shed

with prices for

>   Dead Animal Pit
>   Household Garbage
>   Hazardous Materials

He looked over the pile garbage
in my pickup bed

>   *Twenty Bucks*
the beard shouts at my pile

>   Gary used to only charge me
>   a couple of bucks
I lied

>   *Yah*

well he ain't here anymore

He's in jail

    Tried to blow up the Federal Building in town
the beard says

        Apparently
        the bomb didn't go off
        And the box from the
        PornRodeo he wrapped
        the bomb in
        had his return address on it

        Twenty Bucks
spoke the beard

When Dogs Leave Earth

When Odysseus returned to Ithaca in disguise as a
beggar his loyal dog Argos now old and neglected
recognizes him too weak but to wag a tail and die
as Odysseus hides his tears beneath beggar's rags

People are born
so that they can learn
to live a good life
loving everybody

dogs already know
how to do that
so
they don't
have to stay as long

But when I reach that afterlife
I will surely ask
isn't there another way to work this out
        Lord

do you really have to
put me on earth
to go through this every
six or eight years
adding another
box of ashes
on the mantel
        Next to Argos

Writing Like You Paint

A lot
Away
A little
Away
Working on it a lot
Put it away
Working on it a little
Put it away
Take it out
Put it away
Working on them at once
Several dozen canvases

Several dozen manuscripts
Working on them at once
Put it away
Take it out
Put it away
Working on it a little
Put it away
Working on it a lot
Away
A little
Away
A lot

Walking Top Plate

It was a useful tool
for the foreman
that has had enough
whether
it's another pompous architect
or pimple faced inspector
who has never seen
the ass end of a shovel
in his life

Beginning a conversation with them
he'll slowly starts
walking them to the framing

Careful and cautious
leading to
the ramp that puts you on
the top plate of the framing
ten feet off the ground

As he balances his way
along this thin wooden
line of inches above the
Abyss of sharp penetrating
piles of metal and wood

You'll soon find out
Who
   walks the walk
   or talks the talk

Graves of My Friends

How dare they

wave their flags
In their stupid
flag clown costumes

Like red white and blue
used car salesman

How dare they

Straining to sell
their pitiful patriotism
Over the graves
of true heroes
fallen souls whose eyes
I've looked into

they wave their flags over the
Graves of my friends

How dare they

On Writing

The book
The story that never ends
Why not
Who said the story
has to stay the same

Why not like my paintings
I go back into them
adding or removing something
months
years later

Same for a book
Something I forgot to say
Additional elements
I thought of later
Not having Rachele
killed off in the first chapter
      maybe

you don't ever finish a painting
you just abandon it
like many books abandoned
By keeping Rachele alive for
A few more chapters
      maybe

Over a Bag of Candy

This lame excuse of a human being
that happens to be a legislator
sat there trying to explain
It wasn't his fault
to the
       Live Action News Lady

He just wrote the lame law
that killed this young man

He didn't coward to a bunch of

       Paranoid
       Delusional
       Gun Nut
       Seniors in fear

He didn't mean for that kid to die
       Over a bag of candy

Let That Shit Go

Trying to be mindful
letting things
take their natural course

I tried too hard
to make things happen

Some things you must let go
If you just let that shit go

Then your mind
will become still
like a clear forest pool
in any surroundings

All kinds of wonderful animals
will come to drink at your pool
and you will see many strange
wonderful things come and go

If only you let that shit go

Literary & Artistic Transparencies

All graphics, images, and design elements rights are the sole property of the Lost Cabin Press

Photos
Mountain Spoke a Cloud - *Ophir Peak*
Lahontan Ladies - Sarah Jane, a Lahontan Lady
Going to See a Man About a Horse - *Lover's Cove*

WWW.LOSTCABINPRESS.COM

Poems in the Key of C# is a compilation of poems from the unpublished manuscripts of :

Climbing Barb Wire
Going to See a Man About a Horse
Lahontan Ladies
Your Horses are All Sanpaku
Mountain Spoke a Cloud

Gratiam Magnam
To all those that put me up
And put up with me

www.ingramcontent.com/pod-product-compliance
Lightning Source LLC
Chambersburg PA
CBHW051836170626
46807CB00003B/1213